Illustrations by Blake Doucet

First edition 2024

There once was a boy named Tom who lived with his mom. He was six years old.

Tom lived in a big home full of paintings. His mother owned a large collection that she loved and protected.

The painting's colors
often caught his eye
but his mom always said,
"Don't touch the paintings, Tom.
They're expensive and not for little boy's fingers."

Tom would wait until she walked away and touch them anyway.

He cried and cried and promised never to touch them again.

But this time,

she caught Tom and sent him to his room.

The clock struck twelve and his mother went to bed.

Tom snuck out into the hallway to touch the paintings once again.

His favorite one was a big painting with a giant underwater city.

Fish swirled all around it. His fingers itched to touch it.

Unfortunately, a big "DO NOT TOUCH" sign was next to the painting.

But what did Tom do?

He touched the

painting anyway.

Something weird happened.

His hand didn't touch the canvas

but instead, he felt something wet.

What was going on?

Tom swished and swashed his hand back and forth.

He giggled as the water moved around his hand.

"THIS IS SO MUCH FUN!"

But Tom made a big mistake.

He was having so much fun that he leaned forward a bit too far

and fell into the painting!

Oh no!

What was happening?

Now he was floating underwater!

He tried to kick his legs but they felt strange.

Tom looked down. He had a tail! This was getting scary.

Tom turned around to leave but the painting was gone.

How was he supposed to get home?

He wanted to be safe back in his bed.

At least he had his hat.

Tom wished he had listened to his mom. Maybe touching the painting wasn't such a good idea.

Tom heard someone yelling for help nearby. Maybe if he helped them, he could find his way out!

A giant shark was chasing a mermaid! He swam toward them at full speed. He was terrified but he had to help!

Tom swam with all his might and rammed into the shark's side.

"That'll teach you!"

Big mistake.

Tom ducked and dived around sunken ships, schools of fish, and rocky pillars. The shark wouldn't give up. It followed him without breaking a sweat!

Nearby, Tom saw a rocky crevice big enough for him but too small for the shark. He swam toward it desperate to get away!

The shark's sharp teeth chomped shut.

The bite barely missed his tail fin.

The shark's head was trapped.
It thrashed back and forth,
trying to get free.
Tom retreated farther
into the small cave.

Tom looked up.

A beam of light shone

from deeper in the cave.

A WAY OUT!

The mermaid from earlier waited

for him right outside the cave entrance.

She smiled and waved. "My name is Ella.

Come with me. You will be rewarded for your bravery." Tom nodded and followed.

Tom couldn't believe his eyes.

Ella was leading him toward the underwater city from his favorite painting!

Ella led him right into the main throne room. There, in a chair made of sea shells, coral, and rocks, was the king from the painting. Tom was nervous to meet a king!

"Come here my boy," said the king. "My name is Tritus, and I will grant you one wish for saving my daughter. Anything you desire."

Tom smiled.

This was his chance!

"Mr. Tritus, sir. I would like to go home to my mom. I promise I won't touch any more paintings."

Tritus chuckled and stroked his white beard.

"Your wish is granted, young man."

He waved his trident and a bright

light filled Tom's vision.

Tom sat up in bed and wiped the crusties from his eyes.

Was the underwater adventure all a dream?

But when he lifted the covers, there was a shark tooth sitting in his lap.

Maybe more paintings needed to be explored...

Milton Keynes UK
Ingram Content Group UK Ltd.
UKRC031047151024
449708UK00001B/2

9798330309658